Rally Race

BOOM Kids!

ROSS RICHIE
chief executive officer

MARK WAID
editor-in-chief

ADAM FORTIER
vice president,
publishing

CHIP MOSHER
marketing director

MATT GAGNON
managing editor

JENNY CHRISTOPHER
sales director

SPECIAL THANKS:
Jesse Post, Lauren Kressel, Lisa Kelley and Kelly Bonbright

FIRST EDITION: APRIL 2010

10 9 8 7 6 5 4 3 2 1

FOR INFORMATION REGARDING THE CPSIA ON THIS PRINTED MATERIAL
CALL: 203-595-3636 AND PROVIDE REFERENCE # EAST – 66130

Office of publication: 6310 San Vicente Blvd Ste 404, Los Angeles, CA 90048-5457.

A catalog record for this book is available from OCLC and on our website www.boom-kids.com on the Librarians page.

WRITTEN BY:

Alan J. Porter &

Mark Cooper
CHAPTER 1

Alan J. Porter
CHAPTERS 2-4

ART BY:

Allen Gladfelter
CHAPTERS 1 & 3

Magic Eye Studios
CHAPTER 2

Travis Hill
CHAPTER 4

LETTERS:
Deron Bennett
CHAPTERS 1-2 & 4
Troy Peteri
CHAPTER 3

COLORS BY:
Digikore Studios
CHAPTERS 1 & 2
Rachelle Rosenberg
CHAPTERS 3 & 4

DEISGNER:
Erika Terriquez

COVER BY:
Allen Gladfelter

ASST. EDITOR:
Jason Long

EDITOR:
Aaron Sparrow

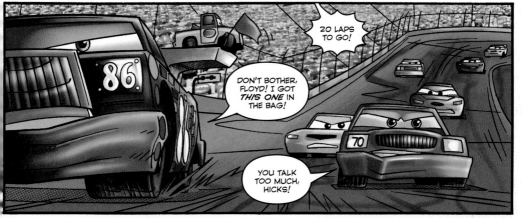

20 LAPS TO GO!

DON'T BOTHER, FLOYD! I GOT *THIS ONE* IN THE BAG!

YOU TALK TOO MUCH, HICKS!

TEN LAPS TO GO

COMING THROUGH BOYS! 4TH PLACE NOW!

I SAY, *THAT* WAS A CHANCY MANEUVER!

HEY BUD, *LOOK OUT!*

HEY BRUSH, MIND IF I *SWEEP* BY TO 3RD PLACE?

JUST KEEP IT CLEAN, AND HOLD YOUR LINE, KID.

FIVE LAPS TO GO

NOW *THIS* IS RACING, FOLKS! IT'S COME DOWN TO CHICK HICKS AND LIGHTNING MCQUEEN, WHEEL TO WHEEL ON THE STRAIGHTAWAY!

MCQUEEN STANDS POISED TO TAKE BACK THIS RACE FROM HICKS, WHO BEAT MCQUEEN AND STRIP WEATHERS FOR THE PISTON CUP LAST YEAR, UNDER WHAT SOME MIGHT CALL "QUESTIONABLE TACTICS".

HEY CHICK, I'M BACK!!

TWO LAPS TO GO

AND THAT'S WHERE YOU'LL STAY, MCQUEEN... *BACK* BEHIND ME! KA-CHIGGA!!

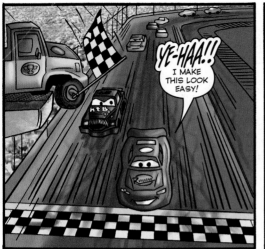

YE-HAA!!
I MAKE THIS LOOK EASY!

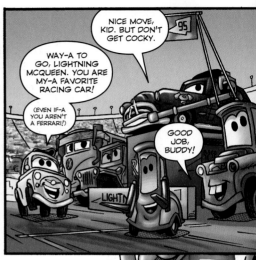

NICE MOVE, KID. BUT DON'T GET COCKY.

WAY-A TO GO, LIGHTNING MCQUEEN. YOU ARE MY-A FAVORITE RACING CAR!

(EVEN IF-A YOU AREN'T A FERRARI!)

GOOD JOB, BUDDY!

LIGHTNING! THIS WAY, LIGHTNING!!

CAN I GET YOUR AUTOGRAPH?

MAKE SURE YOU GET MY GOOD SIDE! DID YOU GET A SHOT OF ME LEAP-FROGGING THE WRECK? WAS THAT CRAZY OR WHAT?

CHICK HICKS SHOULD KNOW I'M GUNNING FOR THE PISTON CUP THIS YEAR!

CAN YOU HEAR HIS SPRINGS CREAKING WITH FEAR? SOUNDS LIKE HE NEEDS A GENEROUS APPLICATION OF RUST-EZE BRAND RIM JELLY! *KA-CHOW!*

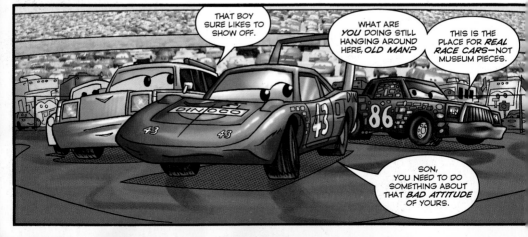

THAT BOY SURE LIKES TO SHOW OFF.

WHAT ARE *YOU* DOING STILL HANGING AROUND HERE, *OLD MAN?*

THIS IS THE PLACE FOR *REAL RACE CARS*—NOT MUSEUM PIECES.

SON, YOU NEED TO DO SOMETHING ABOUT THAT *BAD ATTITUDE* OF YOURS.

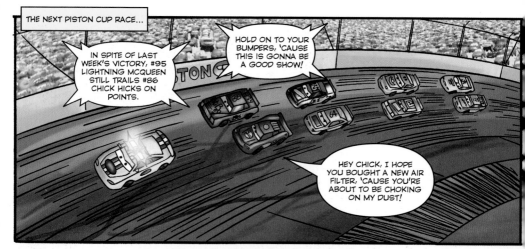

THAT'S A FINE IDEA, HERR MCQUEEN! I'LL BRING MY WHOLE FAMILY!

NOW YOU'RE THINKING LIKE A WINNER! I HAVEN'T BEEN TO RADIATOR SPRINGS SINCE I WAS A KID!

SOUNDS LIKE A GREAT IDEA, LIGHTNING! TELL ME MORE.

THANKS FOR THINKING OF ME, MCQUEEN! I'VE BEEN LOOKING FOR SOMETHING TO DO SINCE I RETIRED!

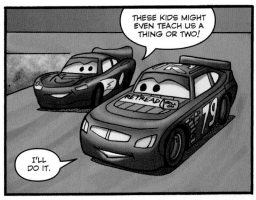

LATER...

GREAT TO *HAVE YOU BACK* IN ACTION, LIGHTNING. THAT WAS A NASTY BLOWOUT.

THANKS, CANDYMAN, IT'S SWEET TO BE BACK.

HEY KID! I HEAR A RUMOR YOU'RE UP TO SOMETHING... SOMETHING *BIG.*

AS BIG AS YOU CAN COME UP WITH, ANYWAY.

I MEAN, A CHARITY RACE? WHAT'S YOUR *ANGLE,* MCQUEEN? PUBLICITY?

IS THIS A PLOY TO SELL MORE MCQUEEN MERCHANDISE?

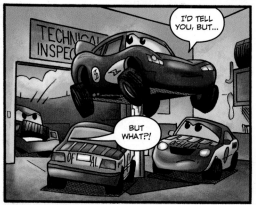

I'D TELL YOU, BUT...

BUT *WHAT?!*

YOU KNOW, CHICK? YOU PROBABLY WOULDN'T KNOW THIS, BUT YOU DON'T NEED TO HAVE AN ULTERIOR MOTIVE TO DO SOMETHING *NICE.*

WHATEVER. YOU GONNA TELL ME WHAT YOU'RE UP TO OR NOT?

WE'RE DOING A CHARITY RACE FOR THE WINNERS CIRCLE KIDS. BUT YOU WOULDN'T BE INTERESTED.

AFTER ALL... THE ONLY THING YOU CARE ABOUT IS *WINNING,* RIGHT?

YOU'LL BE THE ONE IN NEED OF CHARITY AFTER THIS RACE, KID!

I'M SORRY, CHICK...I CAN'T HEAR YOU OVER HOW *AWESOME* I AM.

C'MON, GUYS... CAN WE HAVE ONE RACE WHERE YOU GUYS AREN'T BICKERING LIKE AN OLD MARRIED COUPLE?

YOUR LITTLE RACE WON'T BE MUCH OF AN EVENT WITHOUT THE PISTON CUP CHAMPION IN ATTENDANCE.

YOU JUST CAN'T *STAND* NOT BEING INVITED, CAN YOU?

C'MON, MCQUEEN... ADMIT IT! THIS IS ALL A PUBLICITY STUNT!

DO YOU *EVER* GET TIRED OF BEING A JERK, HICKS?

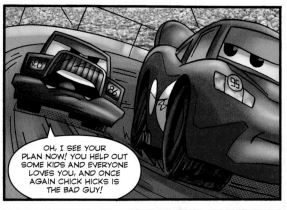

OH, I SEE YOUR PLAN NOW! YOU HELP OUT SOME KIDS AND EVERYONE LOVES YOU, AND ONCE AGAIN CHICK HICKS IS THE BAD GUY!

ARE YOU *LISTENING*, MCQUEEN?!

WOAH, NELLIE! DID CHICK HICKS EVEN BOTHER TO SHOW UP TODAY?

LIGHTNING MCQUEEN SURE DID! IF HICKS PLANS ON DEFENDING HIS TITLE, HE'D BETTER GET HIS HEAD IN THE GAME!

SECOND PLACE *AGAIN!* WHAT WAS HE *DOING* OUT THERE?

NICE WORK, MCQUEEN!

ALL RIGHT, LIGHTNING. WAY TO GO!

YAY!!

BELLISSIMO!!

YAY!! WAY TO GO LIGHTNING!!

LOOK AT HOW EXCITED TIMMY IS. YOU KNOW, I THINK THAT LIGHTNIN'S IDEA MIGHT JUST WORK.

SO DO I, MY DEAR. SO DO I.

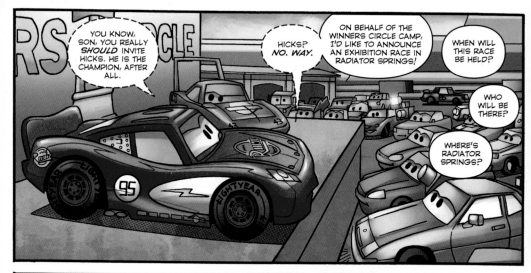

YOU KNOW, SON, YOU REALLY *SHOULD* INVITE HICKS. HE IS THE CHAMPION, AFTER ALL.

HICKS? *NO. WAY.*

ON BEHALF OF THE WINNERS CIRCLE CAMP, I'D LIKE TO ANNOUNCE AN EXHIBITION RACE IN RADIATOR SPRINGS!

WHEN WILL THIS RACE BE HELD?

WHO WILL BE THERE?

WHERE'S RADIATOR SPRINGS?

FREAKIN' MCQUEEN AND HIS RIDICULOUS CHARITY RACE PUBLICITY GRAB...

WHY DIDN'T I THINK OF THAT?!

ERR... EXCUSE ME, MR. LIGHTNING, SIR.

BUT...YOU HAVEN'T INVITED MR. HICKS TO THE RACE...

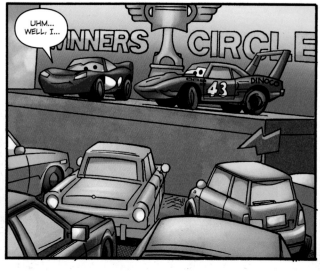

UHM... WELL, I...

EVERYBODY'S WELCOME, RIGHT, MR. MCQUEEN?

ERM... I MEAN... ER...

I'M SURE LIGHTNIN' WOULDN'T WANT TO EXCLUDE *ANYONE*...

SOMETIMES I GET EXCLUDED BECAUSE OF MY LITTLE WHEEL...

...AND I WOULD NEVER WANT *ANYONE* TO FEEL THAT WAY ABOUT OUR CAMP!

YOU'RE RIGHT, TIMMY. EVEN CHICK DESERVES A CHANCE NOT TO BE A—

EVERYBODY'S WELCOME, SON. *EVERYBODY.*

I CAN IMAGINE CHICK GLOATING NOW...

SO *THAT'S* THE BIG SECRET?

OH, LOOK WHO'S HERE. EVERYBODY'S HERO, LIGHTNING "BLEEDING HEART" MCQUEEN!

EXPLOIT ANY KIDS TO FURTHER YOUR CAREER LATELY?

LOOK, CHICK...DESPITE MY BETTER JUDGMENT, I'M *ASKING YOU* TO PARTICIPATE. YOU *ARE* THE PISTON CUP CHAMPION, AND IT WOULD MEAN A LOT TO THE KIDS.

I COULDN'T CARE LESS ABOUT YOUR LITTLE CHARITY CASES, MCQUEEN.

BUT THE CHANCE TO BEAT YOU ON YOUR HOME GROUND?

COUNT ME IN!

HEY, RAMONE *HEARD* THAT, MAN.

IF THAT *JERK* THINKS HE'S GETTING HIS GAS HERE, HE CAN *THINK AGAIN!*

WHAT A *RUDE* CAR!

HEY, THERE'S *NO NEED* FOR THE HOSTILITY, DUDE.

FOR ONCE, I *AGREE* WITH THE HIPPIE.

YOU *JUST WAIT* TILL YOU'RE RACIN' WITH *LIGHTNIN'*.

MA *BEST BUDDY* WILL SHOW YOU WHAT *RADIATOR SPRINGS* IS MADE OF!

I ALREADY KNOW! *FAILURE! HA HA HA!*

HEY, WHERE *IS* MCQUEEN, ANYWAY?

THE NEW RADIATOR SPRINGS SPEEDWAY.

...AND THAT'S HOW WE TRICKED MATER WITH *THE GHOST LIGHT.*

HA HA HA!!

IS THAT A *TRUE STORY,* MR. MCQUEEN?

AW, C'MON TIMMY, NONE OF THAT *MR. MCQUEEN* STUFF. YOU KIDS CAN CALL ME *LIGHTNING.*

AND OF COURSE IT'S A TRUE STORY! WOULD I MAKE UP SOMETHING LIKE THAT?

OH, *I'M SURE* YOU DID.

BECAUSE LET'S FACE IT, MCQUEEN, THERE'S ONLY ONE CAR AROUND HERE WHO'S MADE A CAREER OUT OF *EXAGGERATING—* AND IT *ISN'T ME.*

HEY, CHICK. *WELCOME* TO RADIATOR SPRINGS.

PHAW!!

BOX

htB

86

I'M GLAD YOU MADE IT. THE KIDS ARE LOOKING FORWARD TO SEEING ME RACE AGAINST YOU AND ALL THESE GREAT CARS OVER THE NEXT FEW DAYS.

HA! I HOPE THEY DON'T FALL ASLEEP, WATCHING THAT BUNCH OF HAS-BEENS! NOT LIKE YOU THOUGH, MCQUEEN...

...YOU'RE A *NEVER-WAS!* BWA HA HA HA!

htB

86

I ONLY SEE *ONE REIGNING PISTON CUP CHAMPION* AROUND HERE...

...AND *THAT'S ME!*

GRRR...

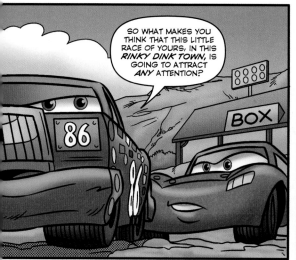

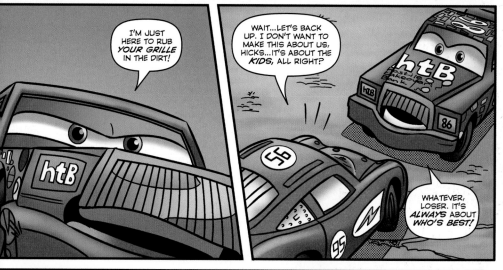

NOW *YOU JUST LISTEN HERE,* MR. HIGH AND MIGHTY PISTON CUP RACER!

YOU CAN *WIN* AS *MANY RACES* AS YOU WANT, BUT CARS LIKE *LIGHTNING* AND *THE KING* WILL *ALWAYS* BE OUR HEROES. THEY USE THEIR FAME TO *HELP OTHERS,* NOT JUST TO LIVE FOR THEMSELVES!

GET LOST, KID. YOU DON'T KNOW A BLASTED THING ABOUT ME.

BOOOOOO!!!!

WOW, TIMMY...YOU SURE TOLD HIM!

SURE DID.

WELL, HE WAS ACTING LIKE A BULLY, AND *I HATE BULLIES.*

STILL...I WONDER WHAT MAKES HIM ACT THAT WAY.

I'M GOING TO TRY AND TALK TO HIM.

WELL, SON, WHATEVER HIS REASONS, YOU STANDING UP TO HIM WAS A *BRAVE THING* TO DO.

YOUNGSTER, IT TOOK *A LOT OF NERVE* TO *STAND UP* TO CHICK HICKS LIKE THAT.

WOW! THE HUDSON HORNET!

DOC.

KING.

GOOD TO *SEE YA,* DOC.

TIMMY, ISN'T IT?

I REMEMBER YOU FROM WHEN MRS. THE KING TOLD US ABOUT THE WINNERS CIRCLE CAMPS.

HOW ARE YOU DOING, KID?

I'M GOOD, *THANK YOU,* SIR!

MAY I ASK YOU A QUESTION?

SURE, TIMMY.

WHAT WAS IT LIKE RACING BACK IN THE *EARLY DAYS* OF THE *PISTON CUP?*

UHMM... WELL...

ER, TIMMY...DOC DOESN'T REALLY LIKE TO TALK ABOUT HIS *PAST.*

...

IT'S OKAY, LIGHTNING.

IN THE *EARLY DAYS* OF PISTON CUP RACING, THERE WEREN'T ANY PURPOSE-BUILT RACE TRACKS LIKE THIS ONE.

WE WOULD RACE WHEREVER WE COULD FIND THE *ROOM*.

THE BIGGEST RACE WAS HELD ON THE SANDS, NEAR WHERE THE BEACHSIDE 500 TRACK NOW STANDS.

SEE YOU GUYS LATER. I TOLD YOU THAT I WAS *NOBODY'S FOOL* WHEN IT COMES TO RACIN' ON SAND.

HORNET, YOU SURE KNOW HOW TO *STING* A GUY.

I WAS A REAL *HUSTLER* BACK IN THOSE DAYS.

SOMETIMES WE RACED ON DIRT TRACKS AT COUNTY FAIRGROUNDS.

THAT WAS A *LONG HOT SUMMER*, WITH RACE AFTER RACE.

I'M GONNA MAKE SURE YOU DON'T SEE THE *COLOR OF MONEY* THIS TIME, HORNET!

YOU GUYS ARE SLIDING AROUND LIKE A *CAT ON A HOT TIN ROOF!*

THEN THEY BUILT THE FIRST OVAL RACE TRACKS.

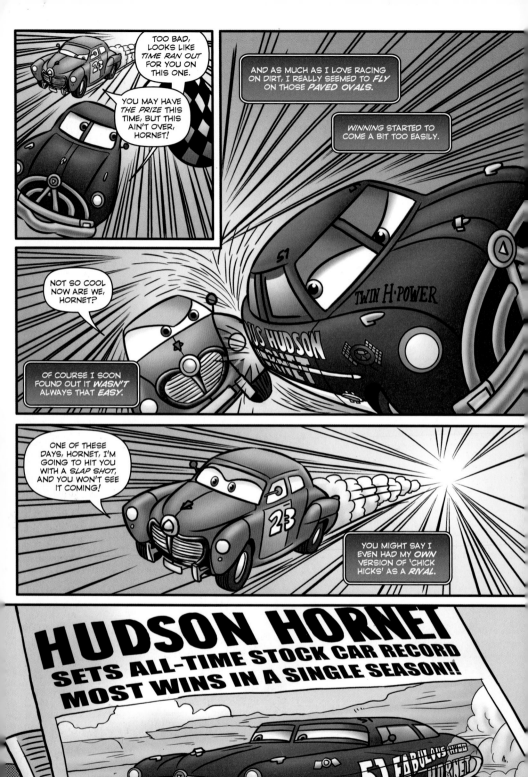

BEFORE I REALIZED WHAT WAS HAPPENING, I BECAME *OBSESSED* WITH *WINNING* THAT CUP.

SOON, IT WAS THE ONLY THING I COULD THINK ABOUT.

CRASH!
HUDSON HORNET OUT FOR SEASON

THEY SAY THAT *PRIDE* OFTEN COMES BEFORE A *FALL*.

IT *DOESN'T* LOOK GOOD.

THEY WERE *RIGHT*.

I'M SORRY, MR. HORNET—BUT THERE IS *NO WAY* THAT YOU WILL EVER RACE AGAIN!

NO! I WON'T ACCEPT THAT. I'LL RACE AGAIN. I'LL FIND A WAY!

IF *THEY* WOULDN'T FIX ME, I WAS DETERMINED TO LEARN *HOW TO FIX MYSELF.*

I *HAD* TO *GET BACK.* RACING WAS *ALL I KNEW!*

BUT I FOUND OUT THAT I COULD ALSO *TEACH MYSELF* ABOUT OTHER THINGS; LIKE HOW *CARS WORKED,* AND HOW TO *REPAIR* THEM.

IT TOOK *A LONG TIME,* BUT I WAS FINALLY *READY FOR MY BIG RETURN.*

BUT RACING *HAD MOVED ON.* THEY HAD *FORGOTTEN* ME. I NO LONGER HAD A PLACE ON THE TRACK.

I THOUGHT I'D DONE A PRETTY GOOD JOB OF IT, TOO...

...UNTIL THE DAY SOME *HOT SHOT RACE CAR* CRASHED INTO TOWN.

I TRIED TO RUN HIM OUT OF TOWN, BUT SALLY HAD OTHER IDEAS...

SCRAPE IT OFF! START OVER AGAIN.

HEY, GRANDPA, I'M NOT A BULLDOZER, I'M A *RACE CAR.*

OH HO— IS *THAT* RIGHT?

THEN WHY DON'T WE HAVE *A LITTLE RACE?* ME AND YOU.

AND BEFORE I KNEW IT, THE ARROGANT LITTLE PUNK HAD ME RACING AGAIN.

DOC, THE FLAG! IT MEANS *GO!*

I DIDN'T REALIZE WHAT WAS HAPPENING AT THE TIME. I WAS GOING TO SHOW HIM UP. HE WAS *ALL SPEED* AND NO CRAFT. ALL I HAD TO DO WAS SIT HIM OUT...

AFTER ALL, I *KNEW HIS TYPE*—HE WAS JUST LIKE I USED TO BE.

NOT THAT I WAS GOING TO TELL *HIM* THAT.

YOU DRIVE LIKE YOU FIX ROADS— LOUSY!

HAVE FUN FISHING, MATER.

SURE ENOUGH, THAT ATTITUDE GOT HIM INTO TROUBLE.

THAT'S WHEN I REALIZED I HAD NEVER GOTTEN RACING OUT OF MY SYSTEM...I WAS LYING TO MYSELF.

I HEAR YOU'VE BEEN SEARCHING FOR THAT LOST RACE CAR?

WELL, HE'S *HERE*. COME *GET* HIM.

I WAS SO *AFRAID* OF FACING MY PAST THAT I *BETRAYED A FRIEND*.

I WAS SO BLINDED BY MY OWN FEARS, I DIDN'T SEE WHAT MCQUEEN MEANT TO THE REST OF THE TOWN. WHAT HE MEANT TO *ME*.

YOU CALLED THEM?

IT'S BEST FOR *EVERYONE*, SALLY.

BEST FOR *EVERYONE?* OR BEST FOR *YOU?*

HE SHOWED ME THAT THE ONLY WAY *TO FACE THE FUTURE*, WAS TO *EMBRACE THE PAST*.

THIS ISSUE OF CARS IS RESPECTFULLY DEDICATED TO THE MEMORY OF
PAUL S. NEWMAN — RACER, ACTOR, GENTLEMAN & THE VOICE OF DOC HUDSON.

KNOCK KNOCK

THE CHANCE TO HUMILIATE MCQUEEN ON HIS OWN TRACK...HOW CAN I RESIST?

HEY, CHICK, WHAT'S THE *WEATHER FORECAST* FOR TODAY?

THE WEATHER?

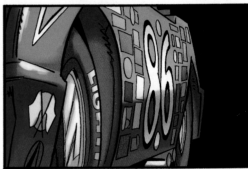

100% CHANCE OF THUNDER!!

KA-CHIGGA! KA-CHIGGA!

THAT TV WINDBAG *CARTRIP* IS ALL EXHAUST THESE DAYS. NO PROBLEM GETTING PAST HIM. 86

ANDRETTI'S STILL FAST EVEN AT HIS AGE. HE'S ONE TO WATCH, BUT HE'S MORE OPEN WHEEL RACER THAN STOCK CAR. 86

EARNHARDT JR. THAT KID'S GOT A LOT OF TALENT, BUT HE ALSO HAS *A LOT TO LIVE UP TO* AND STILL HAS TO PROVE HIMSELF. UNLIKE HIS OLD MAN, HE'S EASY TO INTIMIDATE. 86

AH, *THE GRAND CHAMPION NUMBER FIVE.* HE MAY BE CONSIDERED THE GREATEST IN THE REST OF THE WORLD, BUT HE'S NEVER RACED STOCK CAR STYLE BEFORE. HE'S GONNA LEARN THE HARD WAY THAT HE'S IN CHICK'S WORLD NOW! 86

ANOTHER *OLD TIMER.* I HOPE GRANDPA IS READY TO HAVE HIS DOORS BLOWN OFF. *KA-CHIGGA!* 86

SO, TIMMY...

RADIATOR SPRINGS RALLY

RADIATOR SPRINGS RACETRACK

SARGE'S ARMY SURPLUS

Flo's Cafe

TELL ME A LITTLE ABOUT THE *WINNERS CIRCLE CAMPS* AND WHAT THEY MEAN TO YOU.

WELL MR. CUTLASS, SIR...THE WINNERS CIRCLE CAMPS GIVE US A CHANCE TO HAVE FUN WITH OTHER KIDS!

MY FAVORITE PARTS ARE THE OPPORTUNITIES TO MEET YOUR HEROES AND MAKE NEW FRIENDS!

INSPIRATIONAL STUFF TIMMY, BUT IT SEEMS WE ARE *OUT OF TIME* AND NEED TO GET YOU UP TO THE FLAG STAND, BECAUSE WE'RE ABOUT TO GET UNDER WAY!

SPARK PLUG

FOGGY
WINDSHIELD

LUBEORAMA

THE OIL PAN CAFE

POP N PATCH
TIRE REPAIR

KAFF!
KAFF!

OH YEAH,
*BRING
IT ON,*
BOYS!

THAT'S A
BAD HABIT YOU
HAVE THERE,
MULVILL.

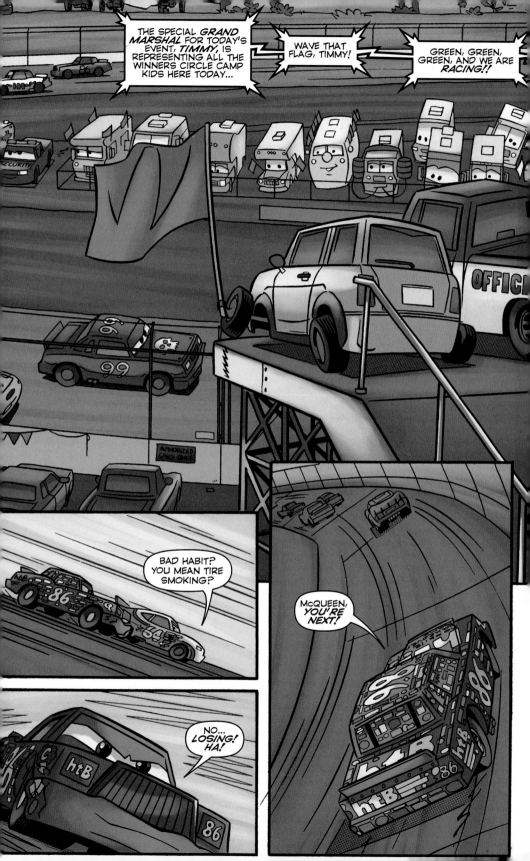

NICE MOVE, MCQUEEN, BUT IT WON'T MATTER... CHICK'S COMIN' FOR YA!

SEE YA LATER, CANDYMAN.

YOU CAN RUN, MCQUEEN...

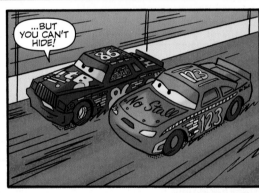

...BUT YOU CAN'T HIDE!

WHAT'S THE MATTER, MR. BIGTIME TV ANNOUNCER? NOTHING TO SAY?

MAYBE YOU'RE GETTING A LITTLE TOO OLD TO RUN WITH THE BIG BOYS, EH, CARTRIP?

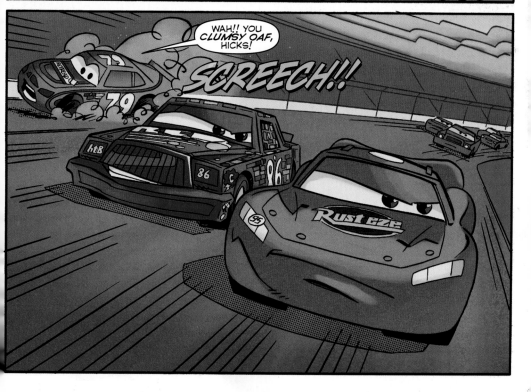

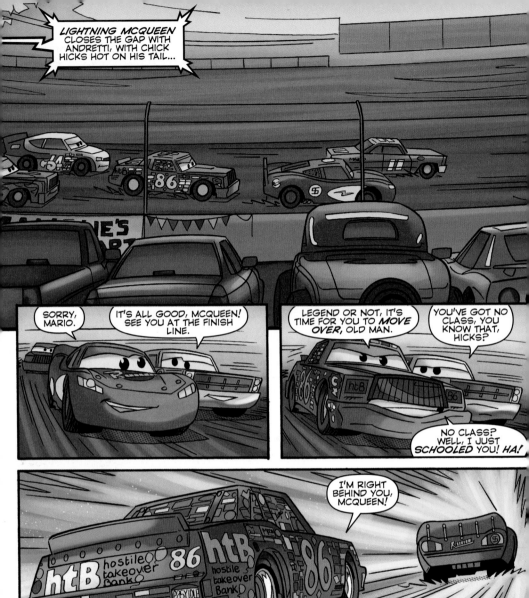

LIGHTNING MCQUEEN CLOSES THE GAP WITH ANDRETTI, WITH CHICK HICKS HOT ON HIS TAIL...

SORRY, MARIO.

IT'S ALL GOOD, MCQUEEN! SEE YOU AT THE FINISH LINE.

LEGEND OR NOT, IT'S TIME FOR YOU TO *MOVE OVER*, OLD MAN.

YOU'VE GOT NO CLASS, YOU KNOW THAT, HICKS?

NO CLASS? WELL, I JUST *SCHOOLED* YOU! *HA!*

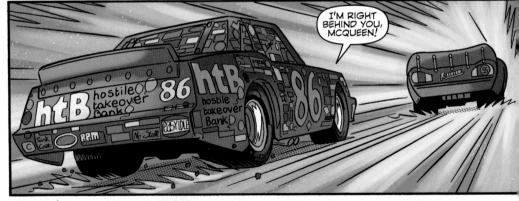

I'M RIGHT BEHIND YOU, MCQUEEN!

OKAY, CHICK, TIME TO GET NEW TIRES. *PIT NOW.*

YOU'VE HAD A STAY OF EXECUTION, MCQUEEN!

FELLAS, LETS **DO THIS RIGHT.** GET THE LEAD OUT!

ON THE WAY!

BOING!

BOING!

≶GULP!≷

BUKOWSKI...

...SIGH.

JUST GET IT TOGETHER AND *GET THAT WHEEL BACK ON.*

ZING!

SKREECH

MISTAKES HAPPEN. LET'S JUST GET FOCUSED. THIS RACE IS OURS TO LOSE, BABY.

TIME FOR SOME *FUN.*

HEY, HOT SHOT, *TOO SCARED TO RACE ME?*

I'LL NEVER UNDER-STAND WHY MCQUEEN LETS THOSE LOSERS HOLD HIM BACK...

...AND TO MAKE MATTERS WORSE, WHY WOULD MCQUEEN REPLACE HUDSON AS HIS CREW CHIEF WITH *THAT BUFFOON?!*

MCQUEEN IS AT *THE BACK* OF THE PACK.

SKREECH

LET'S SEE THE HOMETOWN HERO GET AROUND *THIS ONE.*

BONK!

AAARRRGGGHHHH!!!!

SCREEEEEEE!!!!

ZING!

BONK!

BANG!

AH'M SO NERVOUS AH THINK AH JUST MIGHT BACKFIRE!

PLEASE-A, MATER, CONTROL-A YOURSELF.

NICE TRY, HICKS.

YOU SHOULD SEE A THERAPIST, FIGURE OUT WHY YOU FEEL THE NEED TO DO THINGS LIKE THAT.

WHY DO YOU DO THINGS *LIKE THAT?*

HE NEEDED *HELP,* SIR.

YOU LISTEN HERE, SON... THIS IS A FAMILY OF *WINNERS!*

WE DON'T HAVE TIME TO CODDLE *LOSERS!* THEY'LL ONLY DRAG YOU DOWN, CHICK!

IT'S *WIN AT ALL COSTS.* DO YOU UNDERSTAND THAT?

I--I GUESS SO, FATHER.

POOF!

WHAT ARE YOU, TAKING A *BREAK?* MCQUEEN'S PULLED AHEAD! QUIT DAYDREAMING AND GET BACK IN THERE!

"WIN AT ALL COSTS."

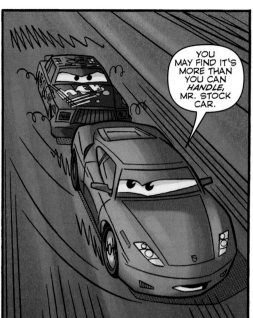

OKAY, SEVEN TIME F1 WORLD CHAMPION... LET'S SEE WHAT YOU'VE *GOT*.

YOU MAY FIND IT'S MORE THAN YOU CAN *HANDLE*, MR. STOCK CAR.

HOW'S THIS, PRETTY BOY? IN THIS COUNTRY, WE CALL THIS *TRADIN' PAINT!*

NOW THAT'S *REAL* RACING!

BANG!

HEY, *HOT SHOT*, HOW ABOUT A LITTLE *BUMP DRAFTING?*

I GUESS YOU COULDN'T HANDLE THE *THUNDER!* KA-CHIGGA!

OUR FIRST RACERS HAVE HIT THE FINAL LAP, AND IT LOOKS TO BE A TWO-WAY BATTLE BETWEEN *CHICK HICKS* AND *THE KING.*

HERE WE ARE AGAIN, OLD MAN.

TOO EASY!

IT AIN'T *OVER YET,* SON.

SURE IT IS, OLD MAN. YOU'RE JUST TOO *SENILE* TO REALIZE IT!

WHAT DID I SAY?

100% CHANCE OF THUNDER!!

YAAAAAY!

YOU KNOW YOU'LL ALWAYS WIN WHEN YOU ROLL WITH THE *THUNDER!*

SEE BRUISER, ALL YOU HAVE TO DO IS LISTEN TO ME, AND YOU CAN OVERCOME ANYTHING.

CONGRATULATIONS, CHICK. LOOKS LIKE YOU BEAT ME ON MY HOME TRACK, JUST LIKE YOU SAID YOU WOULD.

GUESS I GOT TO SEE YOUR *REAR FENDER* FOR ONCE.

YOU *RACE HARD*, HICKS. I'M LOOKING FORWARD TO SEEING HOW YOU HANDLE YOURSELF ON *THE DIRT* TOMORROW.

THE DIRT? TOMORROW?!

DIDN'T YOU LISTEN? THIS WAS JUST THE *FIRST LEG* OF THE EVENT.

TOMORROW WE RACE ON THE DIRT ROADS AROUND THE VALLEY.

YOU MEAN I HAVE TO SPEND *ANOTHER* DAY IN HICKSVILLE, USA?

THANK YOU, MY FRIENDS, FOR THE NEW TIRES. THEY FEEL REALLY GOOD.

NO PROBLEMO, AND WE HAVE-A MORE SPECIAL TIRES FOR YOU FOR TOMORROW'S RACE.

SI.

SO TELL ME, WHAT'S THE SECRET TO WINNING THE BIG RACES?

IT'S NO SECRET, SON. IT'S THE SAME FOR EVERY RACE.

SURE IS. ALL YOU HAVE TO DO IS LEAD ONE LAP.

YEP. THE LAST ONE!

...REALLY, LADIES...

JUST ACCEPT THE COMPLIMENT. YOU'RE ONE FINE LOOKIN' PIECE OF MACHINERY.

≶SNIFF≶ SO HANDSOME. YOU REMIND ME OF STANLEY.

NOTHIN' LIKE SHARING A QUART WITH OLD FRIENDS. THIS SURE BEATS CHASING YOU BOYS AROUND THE BUSH LOOKING FOR MOONSHINE OIL.

YEAH, BUT THOSE WERE GOOD TIMES.

SURE WERE...

SO TELL ME MORE ABOUT THIS ORGANIC FUEL OF YOURS, FILLMORE.

IT WILL MAKE YOUR ENGINE RUN A LOT SMOOTHER, DUDE.

DON'T LISTEN TO THE HIPPIE. THAT STUFF WILL ROT YOUR GAS LINES.

SO HOW DID YOU GUYS GET BIG ENOUGH TO HAUL RACE CARS?

I GUESS YOU COULD SAY WE WERE JUST BUILT THAT WAY.

I THINK YOU COULD LEARN A LOT FROM THESE KIDS, HICKS.

LISTEN, DOC. I RESPECT YOU AS *A RACER* AND *A WINNER.*

BUT YOU *AREN'T MY DOCTOR,* SO *STAY OUT* OF MY PAST. OKAY?

YOU REMIND ME OF SOMEONE I USED TO KNOW.

ON THE TRACK WE WERE *ANYTHING* BUT FRIENDS.

BUT WHEN THE RACING WAS OVER FOR BOTH OF US, WE MADE OUR PEACE.

EARLY THE NEXT MORNING.

MATER? WHAT BRINGS YOU HERE SO EARLY? THE RACE DOESN'T START FOR ANOTHER HOUR.

AH'M S'POSED TO HELP YOU WITH SOMETHIN' IMPORTANT, DOC! AH HOPE YOU REMEMBER WHAT...

...CAUSE AH DON'T!

DO YOU MEAN FITTING ME WITH THOSE SPECIAL DIRT TIRES?

HMMM...DIRT TIRES...DIRT TIRES...

YEAH! AH RECKON THAT SOUNDS ABOUT RIGHT!

WE ALREADY DID THAT YESTERDAY, MATER.

...

SO WE DID! DADGUM!

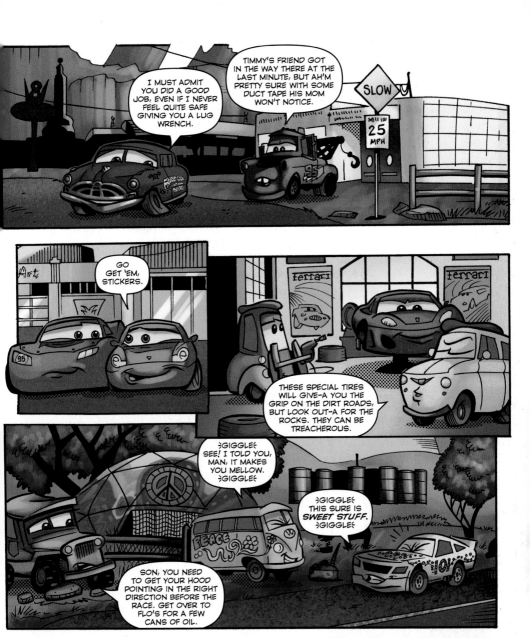

YAY! GO! GO! GO!

AND, THE RACE IS ON!!

OKAY LIGHTNIN'. DOC SAID, REMEMBER TO TURN LEFT TO GO RIGHT, RIGHT?

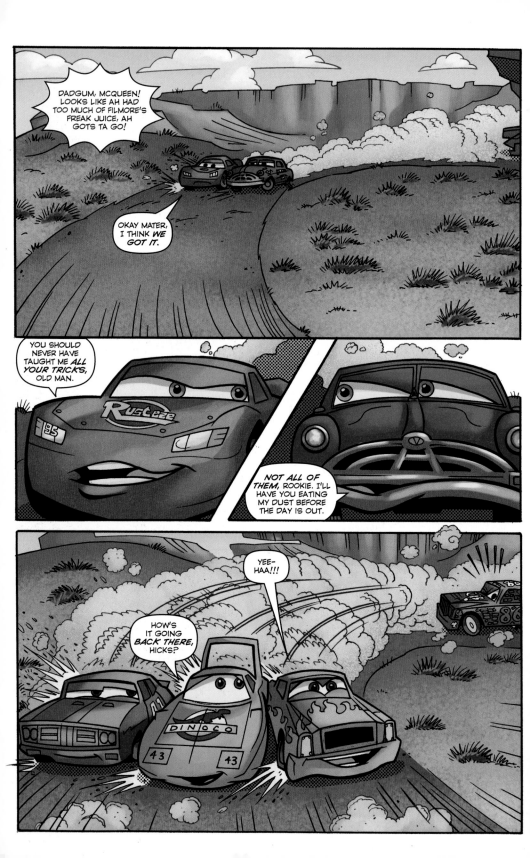

COME ON, OLD MAN, LET'S SEE JUST HOW GOOD YOU ARE ON DIRT.

BE CAREFUL WHAT YOU WISH FOR, HOT SHOT.

LIGHTNING MCQUEEN AND DOC HUDSON CONTINUE TO TRADE THE LEAD.

THIS IS JUST LIKE THE OLD DAYS.

IT'S JUST MISSIN' ONE THING.

YEAH, THE SHERIFF CHASIN' US WITH HIS LITTLE LIGHTS A-FLASHIN' AND HIS SIREN A-WAILIN'!

AH, GOOD TIMES.

THE VETERAN RACERS SEEM TO BE REVELING IN A RETURN TO DIRT RACING...

HEY, MARIO, THIS IS DEFINITELY A LITTLE DIFFERENT FOR ME.

I GREW UP ON DIRT TRACKS, JUST STAY WITH ME. I'LL SHOW YOU A FEW TRICKS.

HAH! FOLLOW YOU? YOU'LL FOLLOW ME!

...WHILE THE ROAD RACE WORLD CHAMPIONS ARE MAKING GREAT PROGRESS.

THIS DIRT JUST GETS EVERYWHERE.

IT'S EVEN IN MY TAILPIPE! HOW DID THEY DRIVE LIKE THIS IN THE OLD DAYS?

THIS IS AN ALL-NEW EXPERIENCE FOR THE CURRENT CROP OF PISTON CUP RACERS.

SPEAKING OF THE PISTON CUP REGULARS, WHAT'S HAPPENED TO REIGNING CHAMPION *CHICK HICKS?* HE IS *NOWHERE TO BE SEEN!*

COME ON, CHICK, YOU CAN DO THIS.

A BENT WHEEL ISN'T GOING TO STOP YOU.

OKAY CHICK, DIG DEEP. YOU'RE A WINNER. REMEMBER THAT. NO ROOM FOR FAILURE.

MAKE THIS WHEEL MOVE!!

THIS IS USELESS!!

MY CAREER IS OVER!

DON'T GIVE UP, MR. HICKS.

IT'S SIMPLE REALLY, ONCE YOU GET THE HANG OF IT.

IT'S THE SAME WAY A SAIL BOAT MOVES. YOU FIRST TACK ONE WAY, THEN THE OTHER TO GO STRAIGHT AHEAD.

DON'T GAS IT, JUST USE A GENTLE THROTTLE TO GET THE WHEEL ROLLING.

I ALWAYS GAS IT—I'M A RACE CAR.

TO DO THIS, YOU NEED A LITTLE FINESSE.

I'M NOT SURE I CAN DO THIS. I ALWAYS ATTACK EVERYTHING FULL OUT.

YES YOU CAN. JUST THINK OF IT AS ANOTHER TYPE OF RACE. A RACE THAT HAS TO BE DRIVEN CAREFULLY. A RACE THAT YOU ARE GOING TO WIN!

WHAT DO YOU KNOW, IT KINDA WORKS!

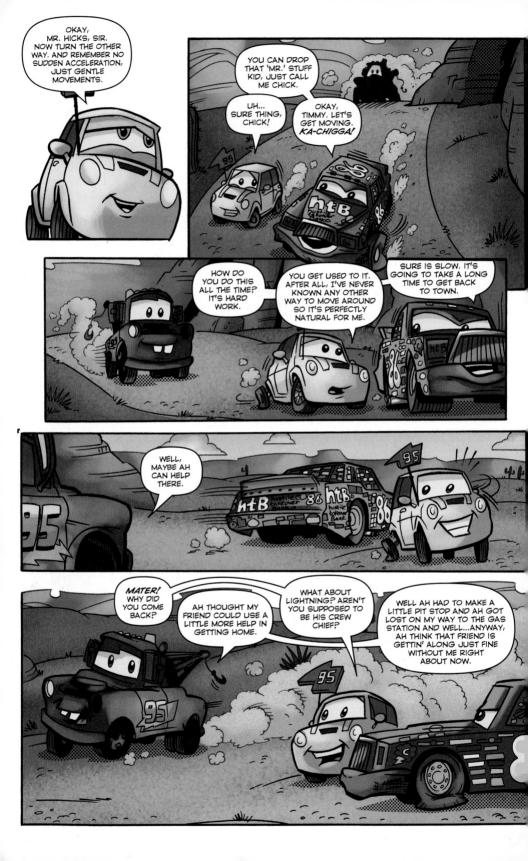

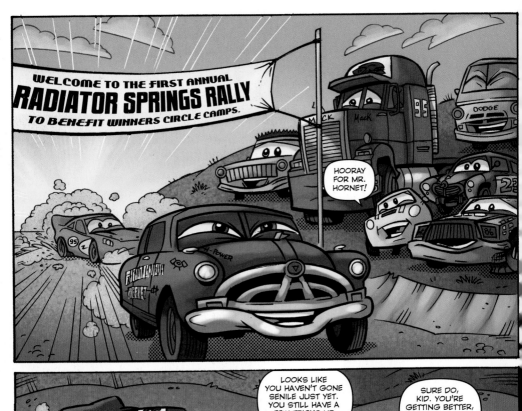

WELCOME TO THE FIRST ANNUAL
RADIATOR SPRINGS RALLY
TO BENEFIT WINNERS CIRCLE CAMPS.

HOORAY FOR MR. HORNET!

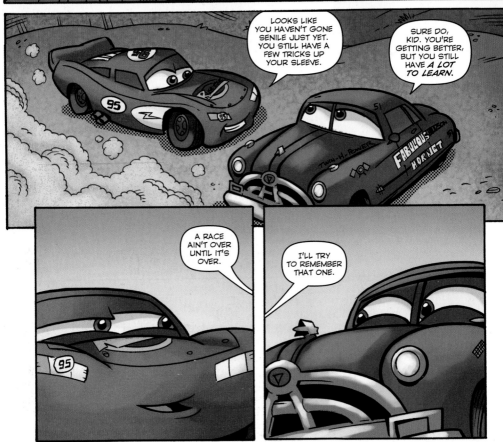

LOOKS LIKE YOU HAVEN'T GONE SENILE JUST YET. YOU STILL HAVE A FEW TRICKS UP YOUR SLEEVE.

SURE DO, KID. YOU'RE GETTING BETTER, BUT YOU STILL HAVE A *LOT TO LEARN.*

A RACE AIN'T OVER UNTIL IT'S OVER.

I'LL TRY TO REMEMBER THAT ONE.

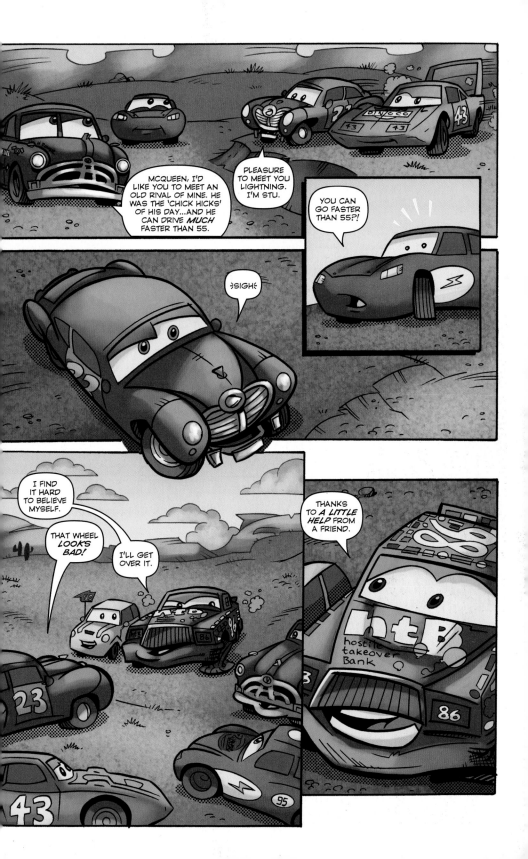

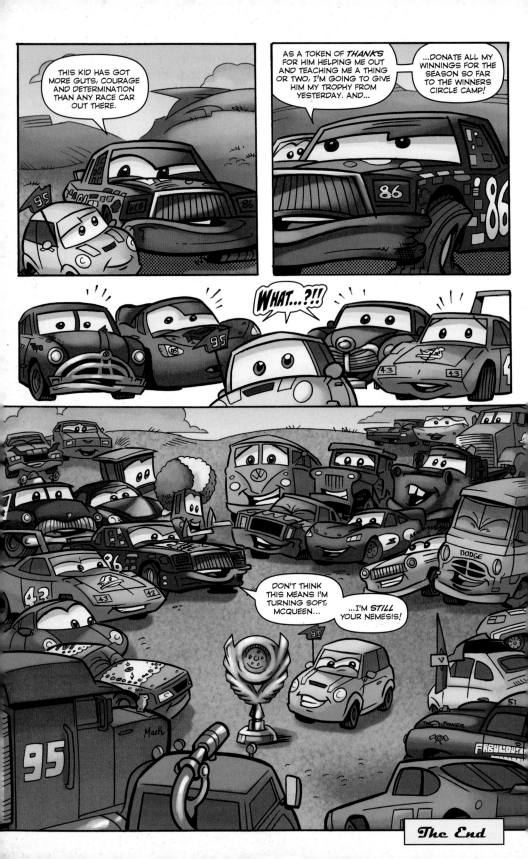

The End

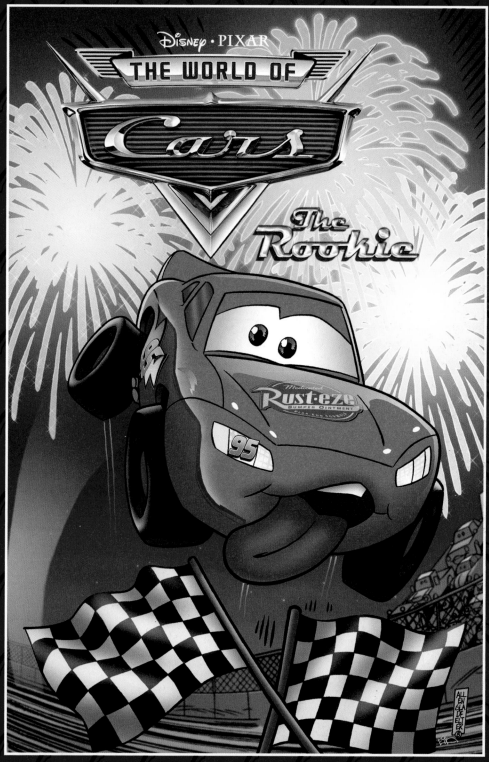

McQueen reveals his scrappy origins as "Bulldozer" McQueen—a local short track racer who dreams of the big time...

CARS: THE ROOKIE
Diamond Code: MAY090749
SC $9.99 ISBN 9781608865024
HC $24.99 ISBN 9781608865284

AND IF ANYONE LEFT A GAP, I'D *GO FOR IT.* 95

I CAN DO THIS!

SKRRREEEECCCHHH

MCQUEEN, YOU *IDIOT!* THERE ISN'T *ROOOOM!*

THE OTHER CARS ALL RESPECTED MY SKILL... 95

...AND MY CONTROL. 95

WOW! THERE WASN'T AS MUCH ROOM AS MCQUEEN THOUGHT THERE WAS!

OOPS! SORRY GUYS!

HEY DUDE! WHAT ARE YOU DOING WITH *MY* NUMBER?!

THEY WOULD SEE ME COMING AND JUST LET ME THROUGH. THERE WAS NO POINT IN CAUSING A CRASH, BECAUSE I *ALWAYS* GOT PAST IN THE END. 95

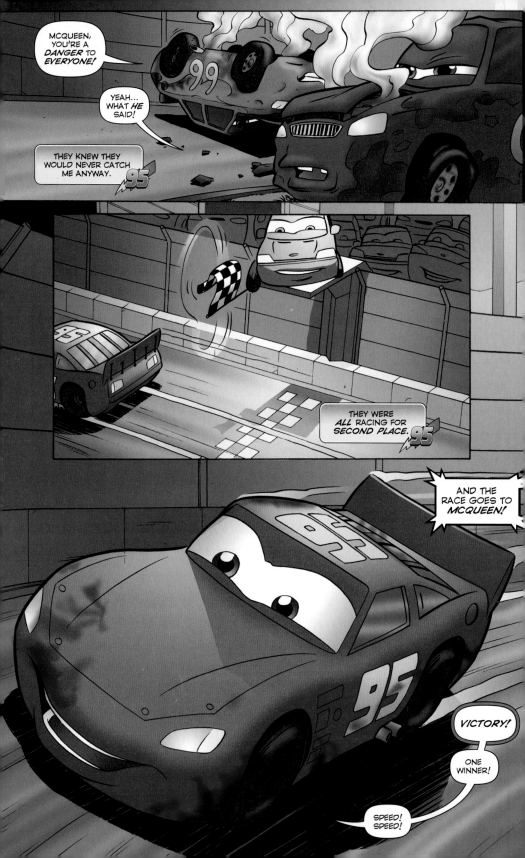

Lightning McQueen realizes that everyone knows his story, but he doesn't know anyone else's! McQueen wants to know how his friends ended up in Radiator Springs... and why they decided to stay.

CARS: RADIATOR SPRINGS
Diamond Code: SEP090701
SC $9.99 ISBN 9781608865024
HC $24.99 ISBN 9781608865284

HAPPY ANNIVERSARY!

CONGRATULATIONS!

DUDES... YOU MAKE AN *AWESOME* COUPLE.

YOU ARE BOTH A GREAT ASSET TO RADIATOR SPRINGS.

A'HMM. YES. CERTAINLY.

YEAH! HAPPY ANDIVERSORY!!

I REMEMBER WHEN STANLEY AND I FIRST MET...

COOLANT

SO HOW *DID* YOU GUYS MEET?

OH *BABY!* THEY WERE *HOT!*

YOU NEVER SAW *NUTHIN'* LIKE IT BEFORE!

THEY HAD FINS THAT WENT *ON FOR MILES.*

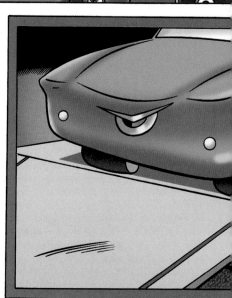

HELL-OO BOYS!

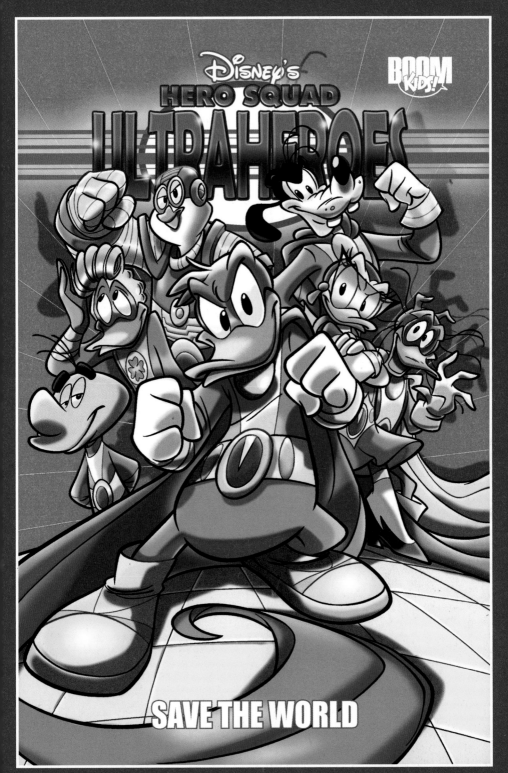

YES! FINALLY!

ULTRAPOD-2 IS MINE!

AND SOON THE WORLD WILL FOLLOW... HUH?!?

STOP!

SLOW DOWN THERE, SUPER-IDIOT!

CRASH

GIVE ME BACK THAT ULTRAPOD, YOU HOVERING HEAP OF TRASH!

YOUR PUNCHES CAN'T HURT HIM!

BUT *HIS* CAN HURT *YOU...*

"*...A LOT...*"

IT'S A BIRD! IT'S A PLANE! NO... IT'S A GOOF!

"*...A WHOLE LOT!*"

グセコツテバピ
マミムピホ
ュヨ干ヱネノ*

*PRETTY MUCH WHAT WAS SAID ABOVE - ABRIDGED AARON

DISNEY · PIXAR
THE INCREDIBLES

FAMILY MATTERS

Mr. Incredible faces his most dangerous challenge yet—the loss of his powers! Is it psychological? Is it an alien virus? Is it just old age?

THE INCREDIBLES: FAMILY MATTERS
Diamond Code: MAY090748
SC $9.99 ISBN 9781934506837
HC $24.99 ISBN 9781608865253

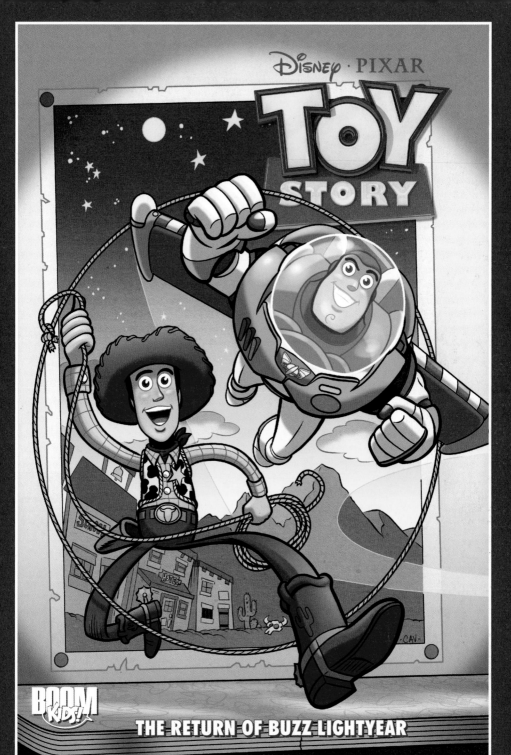

ANDY, HOW MANY TIMES HAVE I TOLD YOU NOT TO RUN DOWN THE STAIRS?!

SORRY, MOM.

WHAT'S A *"GIFT RECEIPT"*? AND WHAT DOES SHE MEAN "RETURN IT AND GET SOMETHING NEW?" YOU CAN DO THAT?!

YEAH, BUZZ...YOU CAN.

THAT JUST SEEMS... *WRONG.*

IT'S LIKE THE POOR TOY NEVER EVEN HAD A CHANCE...

TRUST ME BUZZ...IT'S FOR THE BEST.

"FOR THE BEST?" I THOUGHT YOU'D BE ON MY SIDE.

I *AM* ON YOUR SIDE.

OBVIOUSLY *NOT,* WOODY.

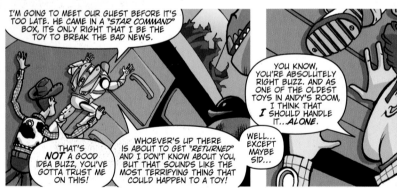

I'M GOING TO MEET OUR GUEST BEFORE IT'S TOO LATE. HE CAME IN A *"STAR COMMAND"* BOX, ITS ONLY RIGHT THAT I BE THE TOY TO BREAK THE BAD NEWS.

THAT'S *NOT* A GOOD IDEA BUZZ, YOU'VE GOTTA TRUST ME ON THIS!

WHOEVER'S UP THERE IS ABOUT TO GET *"RETURNED"* AND I DON'T KNOW ABOUT YOU, BUT THAT SOUNDS LIKE THE MOST TERRIFYING THING THAT COULD HAPPEN TO A TOY!

WELL... EXCEPT MAYBE SID...

COME ON WOODY. STILL SCARED I'M GOING TO STEAL YOUR THUNDER?

YOU KNOW, YOU'RE ABSOLUTELY RIGHT BUZZ. AND AS ONE OF THE OLDEST TOYS IN ANDY'S ROOM, I THINK THAT *I* SHOULD HANDLE IT...*ALONE.*

OF COURSE NOT, IT'S JUST... WELL, YOU DON'T KNOW WHAT'S UP THERE!

YOU'RE RIGHT. THAT'S WHY I'M GOING UP THERE TO FIND OUT!

OH...

TERRAIN LOOKS STABLE. CAN'T DETERMINE YET WHETHER THE ATMOSPHERE IS BREATHABLE. AND THERE SEEMS TO BE NO SIGN OF INTELLIGENT LIFE ANYWHERE.

HELLO!

HALT!

IDENTIFY YOURSELF!

HEY! WHOA THERE SOLDIER!

SORRY! I DIDN'T MEAN TO STARTLE YOU.

MY NAME...IS BUZZ AND THIS IS...ANDY'S ROOM.

I COME IN PEACE.

WERE YOU SAYING SOMETHING? I COULDN'T HEAR YOU OVER THE LASER...

I *SAID*... I COME IN *PEACE!*

AS DO I! SORRY ABOUT THE LASER, FRIEND!

THE NAME'S BUZZ LIGHTYEAR: SPACE RANGER, U.P.U.

THAT'S THE UNIVERSE PROTECTION UNIT.

YEAH... I KNOW. LOOK, YOU REALLY AREN'T SUPPOSED TO BE OUT OF YOUR PACKAGE.

IT'S CALLED A *"STARSHIP."* WHAT'S YOUR DESIGNATION, RANGER?

BUZZ... BUZZ LIGHTYEAR.

WELL, THAT'S JUST GOING TO BE *CONFUSING.* WHY DON'T WE JUST CALL YOU *"SALLY?"*

YOU'VE GOT TO BE KIDDING.

GRAPHIC NOVELS AVAILABLE NOW!

TOY STORY: MYSTERIOUS STRANGER

Andy has a new addition to his room—a circuit-laden egg. Is this new gizmo a friend or foe?

TOY STORY: THE RETURN OF BUZZ LIGHTYEAR

When Andy is given a surprise gift, no one is more surprised than the toys in his room...it's a second Buzz Lightyear! The stage is set for a Star Command showdown!

TOY STORY: MYSTERIOUS STRANGER
SC $9.99 ISBN 9781934506912
HC $24.99 ISBN 9781608865239

TOY STORY: THE RETURN OF BUZZ LIGHTYEAR
SC $9.99 ISBN 9781608865574
HC $24.99 ISBN 9781608865581

THE INCREDIBLES: FAMILY MATTERS

This action-packed trade collects all four issues of THE INCREDIBLES: FAMILY MATTERS. Acclaimed scribe Mark Waid has written the perfect INCREDIBLES story! What happens when Mr. Incredible's super-abilities start to wane...and how long can he keep his powerlessness a secret from his wife and kids?

THE INCREDIBLES: CITY OF INCREDIBLES

Baby Jack-Jack, everyone's favorite super-powered toddler, battles...a nasty cold! Hopefully the rest of the Parr family can stay healthy, because the henchmen of super villains are rapidly starting to exhibit superpowers!

THE INCREDIBLES: FAMILY MATTERS
SC $9.99 ISBN 9781934506837
HC $24.99 ISBN 9781608865253

THE INCREDIBLES: CITY OF INCREDIBLES
SC $9.99 ISBN 9781608865031
HC $24.99 ISBN 9781608865291

THE MUPPET SHOW COMIC BOOK: MEET THE MUPPETS

This hilarious trade collects the first four issues of THE MUPPET SHOW, written and drawn by the incomparable Roger Langridge! Packed full of madcap skits and gags, THE MUPPET SHOW trade is certain to please old and new fans alike!

THE MUPPET SHOW COMIC BOOK: THE TREASURE OF PEG-LEG WILSON

Scooter discovers old documents which reveal that a cache of treasure is hidden somewhere within the theater...and when Rizzo the Rat overhears this, the news spreads like wildfire! Can Kermit keep everyone from tearing the theater apart?

THE MUPPET SHOW COMIC BOOK: ON THE ROAD

With the theater destroyed, the Muppets take their act on the road... but with two very familiar hecklers in every town, will the show be a hit, or will our Muppet minstrels be run out of town in tar and feathers? Also: Fozzie and Rizzo have plans for a big budget PIGS IN SPACE motion picture, but is Hollywood prepared?

THE MUPPET SHOW COMIC BOOK:
MEET THE MUPPETS
SC $9.99 ISBN 9781934506851
HC $24.99 ISBN 9781608865277

THE MUPPET SHOW COMIC BOOK:
THE TREASURE OF PEG-LEG WILSON
SC $9.99 ISBN 9781608865048
HC $24.99 ISBN 9781608865307

THE MUPPET SHOW COMIC BOOK:
ON THE ROAD
SC $9.99 ISBN 9781608865161

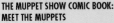

CARS: THE ROOKIE

See how Lightning McQueen became a Piston Cup sensation in this pulse-pounding collection! CARS: THE ROOKIE reveals McQueen's scrappy origins as a local short track racer who dreams of the big time...and recklessly plows his way through the competition to get there! Along the way, he meets Mack, who helps McQueen catch his lucky break.

CARS: RADIATOR SPRINGS

From writer Alan J. Porter, this collection of CARS stories is perfect for the whole family! After his return to Radiator Springs, Lightning McQueen is hanging out with his friends at Flo's V8 Café when he realizes that everyone knows his story...but he doesn't know anyone else's! McQueen wants to know how his friends ended up in Radiator Springs...and more importantly why they decided to stay!

CARS: THE ROOKIE
SC $9.99 ISBN 9781934506844
HC $24.99 ISBN 9781608865222

CARS: RADIATOR SPRINGS
SC $9.99 ISBN 9781608865024
HC $24.99 ISBN 9781608865284

DISNEY · PIXAR
WALL·E

WALL·E: RECHARGE

WALL·E is not yet the hardworking robot we know and love. Instead, he lets the few remaining other robots take care of most of the trash compacting while he collects interesting junk. But when the other robots start breaking down, WALL·E must learn to adjust his priorities... or else Earth is doomed!

WALL·E: RECHARGE
SC $9.99 ISBN 9781608865123
HC $24.99 ISBN 9781608865543

MUPPET ROBIN HOOD

The Muppets tell the Robin Hood legend for laughs, and it's the reader who will be merry! Robin Hood (Kermit the Frog) joins with the Merry Men, Sherwood Forest's infamous gang of misfit outlaws, to take on the stuffy Sheriff of Muppetham (Sam the Eagle)!

MUPPET PETER PAN

When Peter Pan (Kermit) whisks Wendy (Janice) and her brothers to the magical realm of Neverswamp, the adventure begins! With Captain Hook (Gonzo) out for revenge for the loss of his hand, Wendy and her brothers may find themselves in a situation where even the magic of Piggytink (Miss Piggy) can't save them!

MUPPET ROBIN HOOD
SC $9.99 ISBN 9781934506790
HC $24.99 ISBN 9781608865260

MUPPET PETER PAN
SC $9.99 ISBN 9781608865079
HC $24.99 ISBN 9781608865314

FINDING NEMO: REEF RESCUE

Nemo, Dory and Marlin have become local heroes, and are recruited to embark on an all-new adventure in this exciting collection! Their reef is mysteriously dying and no one knows why!

MONSTERS, INC.: LAUGH FACTORY

Someone is stealing comedy props from the other employees, making it difficult for them to harvest the laughter they need to power Monstropolis... and all evidence points to Sulley's best friend Mike Wazowski!

FINDING NEMO: REEF RESCUE
SC $9.99 ISBN 9781934506882
HC $24.99 ISBN 9781608865246

MONSTERS, INC.: LAUGH FACTORY
SC $9.99 ISBN 9781608865086
HC $24.99 ISBN 9781608865338

DISNEY'S HERO SQUAD: ULTRAHEROES

It's the year 2734 and the only one standing in the way of earth's utter destruction is...Mickey Mouse?! Join the four-colored fun as Mickey Mouse, Goofy, and Donald Duck take to the skies to save the world.

DISNEY'S HERO SQUAD: ULTRAHEROES
SC $9.99 ISBN 9781608865437
HC $24.99 ISBN 9781608865529

WIZARDS OF MICKEY: MOUSE MAGIC

Your favorite Disney characters star in this magical fantasy epic! Student of the great wizard Nereus, Mickey hails from the humble village of Miceland. Allying himself with Donald (who has a pet dragon named Fafnir) and team mate Goofy, Mickey quests to find a magical crown that will give him mastery over all spells!

WIZARDS OF MICKEY: MOUSE MAGIC
SC $9.99 ISBN 9781608865413
HC $24.99 ISBN 9781608865505

DONALD DUCK AND FRIENDS: DOUBLE DUCK

Donald Duck as a secret agent? Villainous fiends beware as the world of super sleuthing and espionage will never be the same! This is Donald Duck like you've never seen him!

DONALD DUCK AND FRIENDS: DOUBLE DUCK
SC $9.99 ISBN 9781608865451
HC $24.99 ISBN 9781608865512

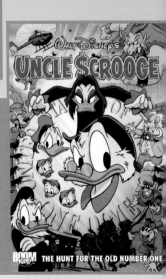

UNCLE SCROOGE: THE HUNT FOR THE OLD NUMBER ONE

Join Donald Duck's favorite penny pinching Uncle Scrooge as he, along with Donald himself and Huey, Dewey and Louie, embark on a globe spanning trek to recover treasure and save Scrooge's "number one dime" from the treacherous grasp of Magica De Spell.

UNCLE SCROOGE:
THE HUNT FOR THE OLD NUMBER ONE
SC $9.99 ISBN 9781608865475
HC $24.99 ISBN 978160886553

THE LIFE AND TIMES OF SCROOGE MCDUCK VOL. 1

BOOM Kids! proudly collects the first half of THE LIFE AND TIMES OF SCROOGE MCDUCK in a gorgeous hardcover collection — featuring smyth sewn binding, a gold-on-gold foil-stamped case wrap, and a bookmark ribbon! These stories, written and drawn by legendary cartoonist Don Rosa, chronicle Scrooge McDuck's fascinating life. See how Scrooge earned his 'Number One Dime' and began to build his fortune!

THE LIFE AND TIMES OF SCROOGE MCDUCK VOL. 2

BOOM! Kids proudly presents volume two of THE LIFE AND TIMES OF SCROOGE MCDUCK in a gorgeous hardcover collection in a beautiful, deluxe package featuring smyth sewn binding and a foil-stamped case wrap! These stories, written and drawn by legendary cartoonist Don Rosa, chronicle Scrooge McDuck's fascinating life.

THE LIFE & TIMES OF SCROOGE MCDUCK VOLUME 1 HC
HC $24.99 ISBN 9781608865383

THE LIFE & TIMES OF SCROOGE MCDUCK VOLUME 2 HC
HC $24.99 ISBN 9781608865420

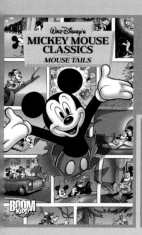

MICKEY MOUSE CLASSICS: MOUSE TAILS

See Mickey Mouse as he was meant to be seen! Solving mysteries, fighting off pirates, and just generally saving the day! These classic stories comprise a "Greatest Hits" series for the mouse, including a story produced by seminal Disney creator Carl Barks!

DONALD DUCK CLASSICS: QUACK UP

Whether it's finding gold, journeying in the Klondike, or fighting ghosts, Donald will always have help with Huey, Dewey, Louie, his much more prepared nephews, by his side! Carl Barks brought Donald to prominence, and it's only fair to start off the series with some of his most influential stories!

MICKEY MOUSE CLASSICS: MOUSE TAILS
HC $24.99 ISBN 9781608865390

DONALD DUCK CLASSICS: QUACK UP HC
HC $24.99 ISBN 9781608865406

WALT DISNEY'S VALENTINE'S CLASSICS

Love is in the air for Mickey Mouse, Donald Duck and the rest of the gang. But will Cupid's arrows cause happiness or heartache? Find out in this collection of classic stories featuring all your most beloved characters from the magical world of Walt Disney! Featuring work by Carl Barks , Floyd Gottfredson, Daan Jippes, Romano Scarpa and Al Taliaferro.

WALT DISNEY'S CHRISTMAS CLASSICS

BOOM! Kids has raided the Disney publishing archives and searched every nook and cranny to find the best and the greatest stories from Disney's vast comic book publishing history for this "best of" compilation.

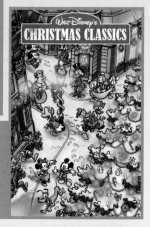

WALT DISNEY'S VALENTINES CLASSICS VOL 1 HC
HC $24.99 ISBN 9781608865499

WALT DISNEY'S CHRISTMAS CLASSICS VOL 1 HC
HC $24.99 ISBN 9781608865482